BARNYARD PURIM

KELLY TERWILLIGER

Illustrated by BARBARA JOHANSEN NEWMAN

This **PJ BOOK** belongs to

_____

_____

PJ Library®

JEWISH BEDTIME STORIES and SONGS

KAR-BEN
PUBLISHING

TO MY BROTHER, R.B.T., MY
EARLIEST ALLY IN GIVING ANIMALS
SPUNK AND SPEECH, THANK YOU!
—K.T.

FOR MY FAVORITE FARM GAL,
JULIA BOYCE.
—B.J.N.

Text copyright ©2012 by Kelly Terwilliger
Illustrations copyright ©2012 by Barbara Johansen Newman

KAR-BEN Publishing
A division of Lerner Publishing Group, Inc.
241 First Avenue North
Minneapolis, MN 55401 U.S.A.
800-4KARBEN

Website address: www.karben.com

Library of Congress Cataloging-in-Publication Data

Terwilliger, Kelly, 1967–
    Barnyard Purim / by Kelly Terwilliger ; illustrated by
Barbara Johansen Newman.
        p.   cm.
    Summary: Farmer Max's animals decide to put on a Purim
play, directed by Chicken.
    ISBN 978–0–7613–4513–8 (lib. bdg : alk. paper)
    [1. Purim—Fiction. 2. Judaism—Customs and practices—
Fiction. 3. Domestic animals—Fiction. 4. Humorous stories.]
I. Newman, Barbara Johansen, ill. II. Title.
PZ7.T2826Ba 2012
[E]—dc23   2011014422

Manufactured in Hong Kong
2 – PN – 10/1/14

021523.5K2/B579

THE PURIM PLAYERS
Directed by Chicken

CAST
Queen Esther.................. Duck
Mordechai...................... Goat
King Ahashuerus.......... Horse
Haman........................ Sheep
Noisemakers................. Cows
Audience.................... Geese

Farmer Max stopped by the barnyard gate.
"Have a good night!" he called to the animals.

"I'm off to a Purim play!"

"I wish I could go, too," said Duck.

"Why does he always leave us here?" sighed Horse.

"Well," said Chicken, "why sit around and mope? Let's put on our own Purim play!"

Everyone began to talk at once.

I've always wanted to act!

Chicken hushed the crowd. "I'll be the director and assign the parts," she said. "Horse, you're the biggest. You should be King Ahashuerus. You're looking for a new queen. So, what do you do?"

Horse looked proud. "I gallop around like crazy!" he said.

"No," said Chicken. "You do not. You invite anyone who wants to be Queen to please come forward."

Instantly, everyone jostled into line, honking and baa-ing.

"Settle down!" ordered Chicken. "King Ahashuerus, you will pick the loveliest—AND QUIETEST—of them all, a Jewish beauty named Esther." She nodded at Duck who blushed and bowed.

Chicken continued. "Now, Esther has a favorite uncle, Mordechai. That's you, Goat! Your beard is perfect for this part!

"When Mordechai visits Esther at the palace, he passes by the King's advisor, evil Haman. Sheep, that would be you.

"Geese, you're the audience, and cows, you'll be the noisemakers!"

"Moo! Moo!" bellowed the cows.
"Nicely mooed, cows," said Chicken "Please do that every time you hear Haman's name."
"Why should the cows moo at me?" asked Sheep with a worried look.

"They aren't mooing at YOU," said Chicken patiently. "They're mooing at evil Haman."
"Moo! Moo!"

Chicken silenced the cows and went on. "Haman is MEAN. He makes all the animals bow to him. But Mordechai holds his head high, because Jews don't bow down. Go on—say it, Goat!"

"I am Jewish, I don't bow down to sheep. I don't bow down to animals, period! It's against my beliefs."

"Well done, Goat!" Chicken bobbed her head approvingly and then turned to Sheep.

"Now, Haman," she said, "you get mad."

"Moo! Moo!" said the cows. Sheep began to cry.

"You don't cry, Sheep! You tell King Ahashuerus that Jewish animals are troublemakers, and he needs to get rid of them. And the king agrees."

"He does?" said Sheep.

"Yes!" said Chicken. "He is a very foolish king. Sorry, Horse."

"This puts you, Duck, in a tough spot. Esther must save her Jewish friends."

"But what if Horse gets annoyed and steps on me?" Duck asked nervously. "He has very big hooves."

"Exactly! But Esther is very brave," Chicken reassured her. "And smart. You make a plan to stop mean old Haman."

The cows mooed, and Sheep began to cry again. "I'm NOT mean!" he whimpered.

"He needs a costume to help him pretend," said Goat. "Come on, Sheep. Let's find you something scary."

"I hope Goat's plan works," said Chicken. "We can't have our bad guy crying all the time."

Chicken turned to Duck. "Queen Esther, you invite the King and Haman to a special supper. Goat, are you almost ready with Sheep's costume?"

"Almost!" called Goat from the barn.

Just then a figure slunk into
the barnyard. The cows were
so startled, they forgot to moo.
Everyone stared. Only Horse, who
seemed to have lost interest in the
play, continued to chew his oats.

"Wow! Look at that fox costume!" whispered a goose.

"He looks great," a cow agreed.

The fox stared at Duck. Duck shivered.

Chicken cleared her throat. "When Haman arrives for dinner, Esther is very nervous, but she must go through with her plan. Go on, Duck. Show us how brave Esther is!"

Duck took a deep breath. "Haman!" she said bravely, though her voice quivered. "Come in. Make yourself comfortable. The King will be here soon."

Fox circled Duck, moving closer and closer. He was no longer a weepy Sheep. He looked like a fox. He moved like a fox. He looked ready to pounce. The geese in the audience were impressed. This was what acting was all about!

"Ahashuerus! Haman is here. Supper is ready," Duck called anxiously, but Horse didn't answer.

Duck peered at the crouching Haman. His costume was incredible. But where were the snaps? Where were the ties? Haman opened his mouth. Duck saw a long, pink tongue...and sharp teeth! This was no costume!

The fox sprang. Duck fluttered out of reach. "Help! Help!" she quacked.
"Ahashuerus!" she screamed at Horse. "Haman is going to eat me up!"
"Good acting job!" Chicken shouted. The geese applauded.
The fox lunged.

"Ahashuerus, wake up!" cried Duck in a panic. "Haman is a REAL fox! He is going to eat us all!"

"What?" said Horse, tossing his head.

The fox bared his teeth. The animals backed away in confusion. It WAS a real fox!

Just then, Sheep dashed into the barnyard, wearing an old wolf costume and snarling. "Here I am everybody!" he cried. He stopped and glared at the fox. "Hey! Take off that costume! This is MY part!"

The fox paid no attention. His eyes were still on Duck. Trying to act as brave as Queen Esther, Duck flapped her wings and ran at the fox. "How dare you sneak in here and try to attack me!" she quacked. "Scram! And never come back!"

The whole barnyard went into action. Horse whinnied and reared. Chicken pecked. Goat lowered his horns. Geese honked. The cows mooed.

Startled, the fox turned and ran. First there was silence. Then everybody cheered. "Long live Queen Esther! Esther saved the day!"

"What's happening?" said Sheep, tugging off the head of his wolf costume.

"I'm so confused," said Horse.

"Don't worry," said Chicken. "You're King Ahashuerus, and he's always confused."

Everybody laughed.

They were still laughing, and dancing, and singing when
Farmer Max came home. carrying a basket of hamantaschen.

ABOUT PURIM

Purim, a holiday that comes in early spring, recalls how brave Queen Esther saved the Jewish people of Persia from wicked Haman's evil plot to destroy them. The story is recounted in the Biblical book of Esther. Families celebrate by wearing costumes, listening to the reading of the Megillah (a scroll containing the story) and making noise with groggers, blotting out the name of the villain Haman.

ABOUT THE AUTHOR AND ILLUSTRATOR

Kelly Terwilliger is a resident storyteller for Oregon elementary schools, as well as a poet and artist. She received a B.A. in English Literature from Swarthmore College, and an M.A. in Literature from the University of Wisconsin. She lives in Eugene, Oregon, with her husband and children. Her books include *Bubbe Isabella and The Sukkot Cake* (Kar-Ben).

Barbara Johansen Newman lives in Boston with her husband, three sons, and a French Bulldog named Bitty. She spends her time writing and illustrating children's books, painting, designing fabrics, or wishing that she really could have farm animals, especially a goat or a duck.